LEGO® DC Super Heroes: Last Laugh! (978-0-545-48029-1) © 2015 The LEGO Group.™ & © DC Comics. (s15)
LEGO® DC Super Heroes: Save the Day! (978-0-545-48028-4) © 2015 The LEGO Group.™ & © DC Comics. (s15)
LEGO® DC Super Heroes: Space Justice! (978-0-545-82556-6) © 2015 The LEGO Group.™ & © DC Comics. (s15)
LEGO® DC Super Heroes: Friends and Foes! (978-0-545-78504-4) © 2015 The LEGO Group.™ & © DC Comics. (s15)

ISBN 978-0-545-92622-5

10 9 8 7 6 5 4 3 2 1   15 16 17 18 19

Printed in China   38
First printing 2015

Book design by Erin McMahon

FLYING OVER METROPOLIS IS A HERO WHO CAN LEAP BUILDINGS IN A SINGLE BOUND, LIFT CARS ABOVE HIS HEAD, FREEZE CROOKS WITH HIS BREATH, AND HEAR THINGS MILES AWAY.
THIS IS THE WORLD'S PROTECTOR. THIS IS SUPERMAN!
HELP!
SOUNDS LIKE SOMEONE NEEDS MY HELP.

AFTER WRECKING BANE'S TUMBLER, BATMAN SWOOPS IN TO STOP THE COLD CRIMINALS.
WHAP!
YOU'RE RUINING ALL OF OUR FUN!
YOU SHOULD HAVE THOUGHT OF THAT BEFORE YOU MESSED WITH MY FRIENDS.
OH, AND STEALING MONEY IS BAD, TOO!

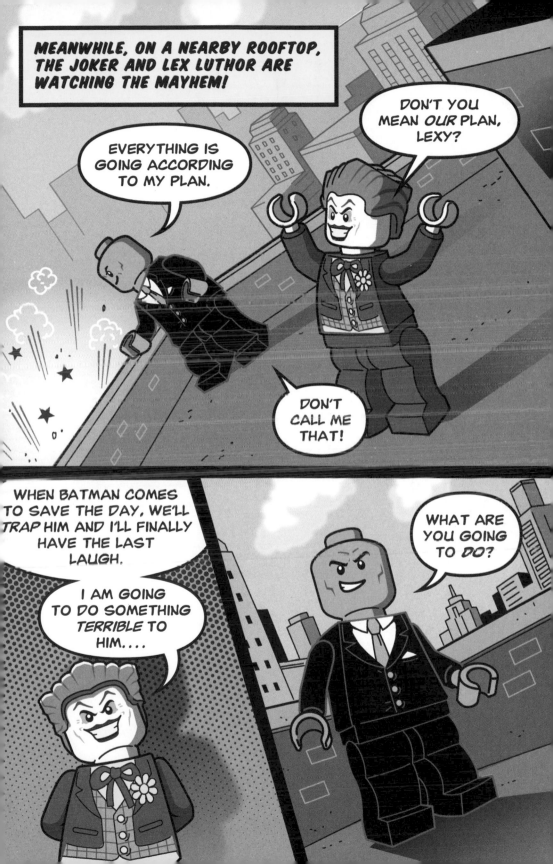

HERE'S A RIDDLE— WHO WEARS BLACK AND ANNOYS ALL THE CROOKS IN GOTHAM CITY?

IT WASN'T A JOKE, IT WAS A *RIDDLE*!

YOU'RE NOT VERY FUNNY, RIDDLER. WHY DON'T YOU LEAVE THE JOKES TO ME?

BATMAN SWINGS IN FOR THE RESCUE, BUT MR. FREEZE USES HIS FREEZE GUN TO STOP BATMAN.

YOU CAN'T STOP BAT—

BRRRZZZZZTTTTTTTTTT000

—MAN?

KLUNK!!

NICE RESCUE.

BATMAN IS ALL ICED UP. CAN HE ESCAPE IN TIME?

ROBIN STAYS AND HELPS THE PEOPLE AT THE BANK, WHILE BATMAN GOES AFTER BANE AND IVY IN THEIR TUMBLER.

THE CRIMINALS TRY TO SHOOT BATMAN OUT OF THE SKY, BUT HE'S TOUGH TO CATCH.

CHOOOM!!!

CHOOOM!!!

EAT MISSILES, BATMAN!

BATMAN DODGES THE MISSILES, AND THEN LEAPS FROM HIS VEHICLE.

TURN YOURSELVES IN, CRIMINALS. . . .

YOU CAN'T OUTRUN A BAT!

SSSNNNOOORR...

OOEEEESHHHH!!...

SLAM!

THE JOKER IS GOTHAM CITY'S WORST NIGHTMARE. SOMETIMES HE USES POISON GAS. OTHER TIMES HE USES TOY BOMBS. BUT IF HE USES THIS PIE ON THE PEOPLE OF GOTHAM CITY—HE'LL RUIN DESSERT FOR EVERYONE! THEY'LL BE WASHING CREAM PIE OUT OF THEIR HAIR FOR MONTHS. WHO WILL SAVE THE DAY?

CORRECTION, HARLEY QUINN. BATMAN AND *FRIENDS!*
BATMAN. CATWOMAN. ROBIN. SUPERMAN. TOGETHER, CAN ANYONE DEFEAT THESE POWERFUL HEROES?

WHEN THE WORLD IS IN TROUBLE, IT CAN COUNT ON HEROES TO SAVE THE DAY!

WHEN LEX LUTHOR AND GORILLA GRODD TEAM UP, SO DO SUPERMAN AND BATMAN. THEY WORK TOGETHER TO TAKE DOWN THE VILLAINS AND HELP THOSE IN DANGER.

BETWEEN MISSIONS, THE HEROES HANG OUT AT THEIR SECRET HEADQUARTERS. WHEN THEY AREN'T FIGHTING BAD GUYS, THEY LIKE TO HAVE FUN.

HAS ANYONE SEEN MY BEACH UMBRELLA?

"IF THERE'S AN EMERGENCY, REMEMBER: IT'S NOT ABOUT WORKING FAST, IT'S ABOUT WORKING SMART!" SUPERMAN REMINDS THEM.

THE HEROES' MOVIE IS CUT OFF BY A MESSAGE FROM THREE SPACE SUPER-VILLAINS: DARKSEID, SINESTRO, AND BRAINIAC. "WE WILL ATTACK YOUR PLANET—UNLESS EVERYONE ON EARTH SENDS US ALL THEIR TOYS. YOU HAVE 24 HOURS!"

ALL OF OUR TOYS?! THOSE VILLAINS!

THE VILLAINS ARE TOUGHER THAN THE HEROES THOUGHT. ARROWS CAN'T GET THROUGH SINESTRO'S SHIELD. DARKSEID IS AS STRONG AS SUPERMAN.

AND BRAINIAC IS . . . WELL, BRAINY! THE HEROES DIDN'T STAND A CHANCE WITHOUT A PLAN.

"BUT FIRST, WE NEED A PLAN," SAYS BATGIRL.

WORKING TOGETHER, THE THREE HEROES COME UP WITH A VERY SMART PLAN.

WHEN THE SPACE ALIEN OPENS THE BOX, HE GETS A HERO-SURPRISE. EVERYTHING IS GOING ACCORDING TO THE PLAN.

NEXT, SUPERGIRL PUTS A SHEET OVER HER HEAD AND SNEAKS UP ON SINESTRO. WHEN HE GETS SCARED, HIS RING LOSES POWER.

AFTER THAT, WONDER WOMAN TAKES CARE OF SINESTRO. NOW THE OTHER HEROES ARE FREE. "WHAT A GREAT COSTUME!" SAYS HAWKMAN.

"WHAT A GREAT PLAN!" SAYS GREEN ARROW.

THE HEROES HAVE BEEN SAVED AND THE VILLAINS HAVE BEEN DEFEATED ALREADY. "WAIT A MINUTE," SAYS SUPERGIRL, "WEREN'T THERE *THREE BAD GUYS?*"

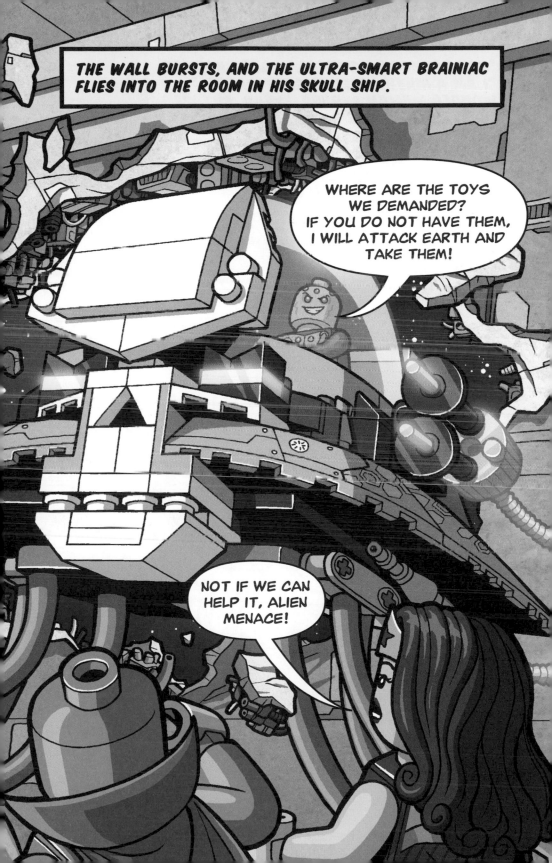

THE HEROES WORK TOGETHER—USING THEIR BRAINS AND MUSCLES AGAINST BRAINIAC!

GREEN LANTERN USES HIS POWER RING TO FLY THE VILLAINS TO SPACE JAIL.

"ARE THERE TOYS IN SPACE JAIL?" DARKSEID ASKS. "ONLY IF YOU BEHAVE," GREEN LANTERN ANSWERS.

WHEN THE HEROES GET HOME, THEY NEED A GOOD REST. HAVING A SPACE ADVENTURE AND SAVING THE WORLD IS HARD WORK!

ZZZZZZZZZZZZZZZ

LATER, SUPERMAN AND BATMAN ARRIVE HOME. "EVERYONE'S ASLEEP. I GUESS THERE WEREN'T ANY EMERGENCIES TODAY," SAYS SUPERMAN.

SNORE

"NOPE," SAYS BATMAN. "I GUESS WE DIDN'T MISS ANYTHING—EXCEPT NAP TIME."

GOTHAM CITY IS IN TROUBLE AGAIN. IT'S A GOOD THING BATMAN IS ALWAYS THERE TO SAVE THE DAY!

THIS IS WHAT HAPPENS WHEN YOU ACT LIKE AN ANIMAL.

BEFORE BATMAN GETS FAR, HIS PHONE RINGS . . .

"YEESH," BATMAN SAYS, "THAT'S A LOT OF STUFF FOR ONE GUY TO HANDLE ALONE."

"YOU DON'T HAVE TO HANDLE IT ALONE," SAYS
SUPERMAN.
"THAT'S WHAT FRIENDS ARE FOR!" SAYS
WONDER WOMAN.

"BATMAN AND I AREN'T REALLY FRIENDS. HE'S MORE LIKE MY BOSS," SAYS BATGIRL, "BUT I CAN HELP, TOO."

"I DON'T NEED YOUR HELP," BATMAN SAYS. "I'VE BEEN PUTTING CROOKS IN JAIL SINCE I WAS IN GRADE SCHOOL!"

"YEAH, WELL, I'VE BEEN KNOCKING OUT BAD GUYS SINCE I WORE PAJAMAS!" SAYS SUPERMAN.

SUPERMAN AND BATMAN TAKE TO THE SKY IN A RACE TO FIND THE SUPER-VILLAINS. THE JOKER IS A DANGEROUS CLOWN, AND DARKSEID IS AN ALIEN THREAT FROM OUTER SPACE! BUT WHERE COULD THEY BE?

WONDER WOMAN SIGHS. "YOU KNOW IT'S UP TO US TO SAVE THE CITY, RIGHT?"

"YUP," SAYS BATGIRL. "WE BETTER GET STARTED—WE HAVE A LOT TO DO!"

FIRST, WONDER WOMAN CAPTURES ALL THE VILLAINS WHO ESCAPED FROM ARKHAM ASYLUM IN HER INVISIBLE JET. BANE, SCARECROW, AND POISON IVY CAN'T ESCAPE FROM HER GOLDEN LASSO OF TRUTH!

THEN, BATGIRL STOPS THE CROOKS FROM ROBBING THE BANK. THE RIDDLER, LEX LUTHOR, AND HARLEY QUINN DON'T STAND A CHANCE AGAINST BATGIRL'S MARTIAL ARTS SKILLS.

TOGETHER, WONDER WOMAN AND BATGIRL CAPTURE BLACK MANTA, SINESTRO, AND CAPTAIN COLD BEFORE THEY CAN ROB THE MUSEUM.

MEANWHILE, SUPERMAN AND BATMAN HAVE FOUND THE SUPER-VILLAINS! THE JOKER IS WRECKING THE CITY ZOO IN HIS STEAMROLLER! AND DARKSEID IS EATING COMMISSIONER GORDON'S MISSING LUNCH!

BATMAN AND SUPERMAN ARGUE OVER WHO SHOULD SAVE THE CITIZENS AND WHO SHOULD CAPTURE THE VILLAINS. THEY CAN'T AGREE, SO INSTEAD, THEY BOTH END UP PITCHING A TANTRUM.

WHILE THEY'RE DISTRACTED, DARKSEID SHOOTS A BEAM OF RED ENERGY FROM HIS EYES AND ZAPS THE SUPER HEROES. THEY ARE KNOCKED OUT! "NOW, THAT'S FUNNY!" THE JOKER LAUGHS. "YOU SHOULD HAVE ATTACKED US BAD GUYS WHEN YOU HAD THE CHANCE, SILLY HEROES."

REALIZING HOW THEY GOT HERE, THE HEROES DECIDE TO MAKE THINGS RIGHT. "SORRY FOR THE WAY I ACTED," SAYS BATMAN. "I NEED TO LEARN HOW TO WORK BETTER AS PART OF A TEAM."

"I'M SORRY, TOO," SAYS SUPERMAN. "I GUESS I SHOULD LEARN TO SHARE THE VILLAINS."

"THERE THEY GO AGAIN," SAYS BATGIRL.
"WANT TO GO GET SOME ICE CREAM?" ASKS WONDER WOMAN.
"YES, PLEASE!" SAYS BATGIRL. "BUT LET'S LEAVE THE BOYS HERE."